And My Mean Old Mother Will Be Sorry,

BLACKBOARD BEAR

For Kimi

Second edition 2000

Library of Congress Cataloging-in-Publication Data

Alexander, Martha.
And my mean old mother will be sorry, Blackboard Bear / Martha Alexander. — 1st ed.
p.   cm.
Summary: When his mother gets angry over the mess he has made and he decides
to run away with his friend, Blackboard Bear,
Anthony discovers that the woods can be a very scary place.
ISBN 0-7636-0668-5
[1. Runaways — Fiction. 2. Bears — Fiction.] I. Title.
PZ7.A7765An 1999
[E] — dc21   98-14047

2 4 6 8 10 9 7 5 3 1

Printed in Hong Kong

This book was typeset in Stempel Schneidler Roman.
The illustrations were done in colored pencil and watercolor.

Candlewick Press
2067 Massachusetts Avenue
Cambridge, Massachusetts 02140

And My Mean Old Mother Will Be Sorry,
BLACKBOARD BEAR

Martha Alexander

CANDLEWICK PRESS
CAMBRIDGE, MASSACHUSETTS

Boy, is she mad! Let's get out of here!

No more honey? Me neither. I'm full.

EEEEEEEEK!
Sticky honey all over
the kitchen! A little boy named
Anthony better be in bed—
that's all I can say!

Mean old mother! Always yelling!
It makes me so mad!

Can't ever have any fun in this house.

What? Run away? You and me?

We could live in a cave? That's great!
Let's go! No, I don't want to take my toothbrush.

I'll *never* brush my teeth again.
And my mean old mother will be sorry.

These blueberries are really good, but I'm still hungry.
Honey? Oh, yes, I love honey.

My mom *never* lets me eat this much, though.
She says I'd get sick.

Oh, no, I'm not sick. I think my stomach just feels this way from walking so far.

That's better. Do you think we could
find a hamburger somewhere?

No hamburger . . . just fish?
Oh, yes, I like trout.

But I don't think I can eat it
while it's wiggling.

Oh! You don't mind the wiggling?
Well, maybe I *could* get used to it.

Maybe I'll get used to the dark too,
but I wish I had my flashlight.

You're sure it's only an owl?
Oh, no, I'm not afraid.

Am I getting sleepy?
Well, yes, a little.

This is a great cave!
But what is that fluttering noise?
Oh, I didn't know bats live in caves too.
Couldn't we have a cave of our own?
Not tonight? Oh.

I wish I had my pillow.
I'm a little cold.
You'll keep me warm?
Oh, that's better.
I think I'll get my pillow and
blanket in the morning.
Maybe my bed too.

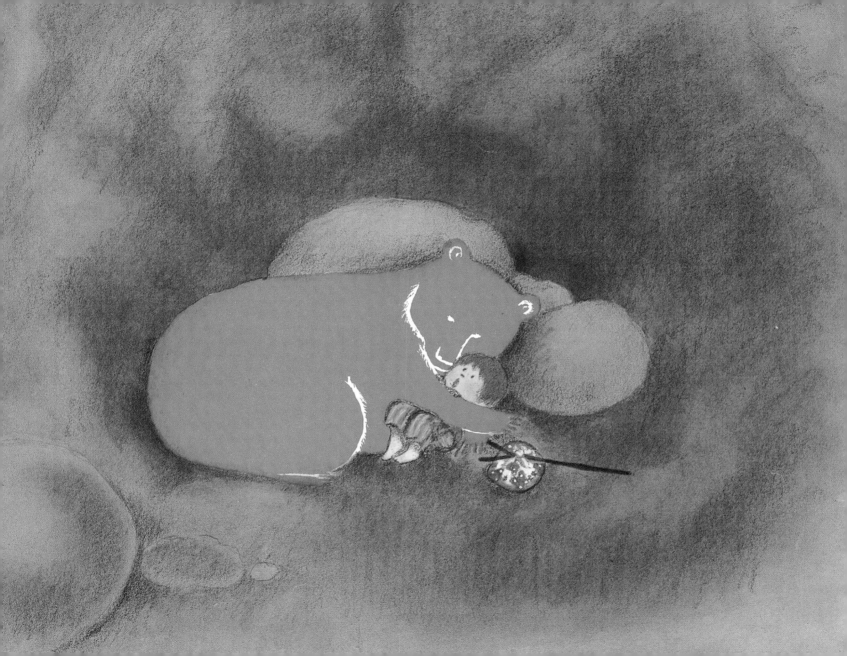

Miss me? You really think she would?
I don't want her to be lonesome.
She's mostly a good mom.
You mean go back? Well, maybe.
We'll talk about it in the morning.
Good night.

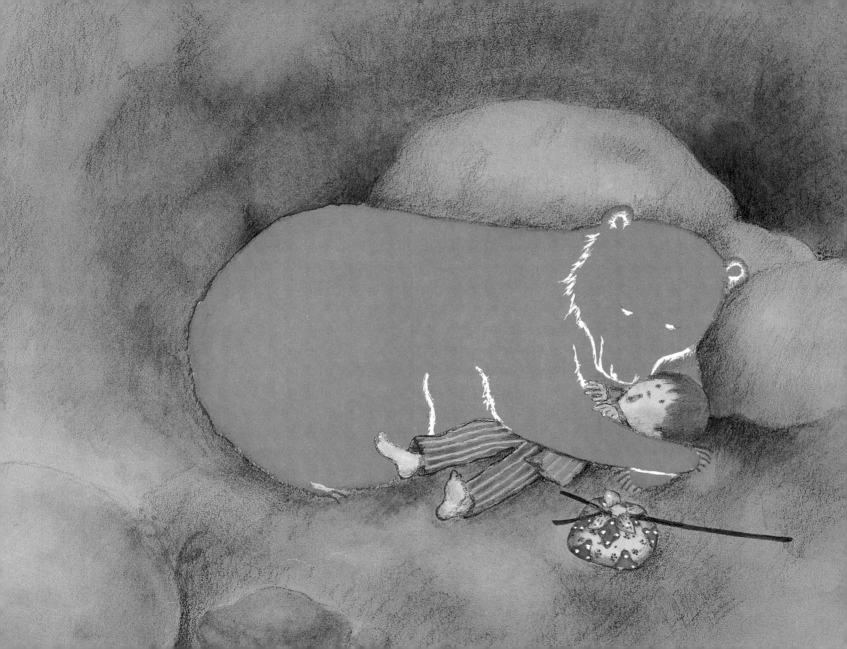

It's almost light, and I'm getting hungry. Berries for breakfast again? No orange juice or cereal?

You *really* think I should go home?
But I could visit you often, couldn't I? Oh, good.

Good-bye. Thanks for the ride back.
I'll be seeing you.

Hello, Teddy! You really did?
You missed me a lot?

I love you too, Teddy.